# WHISKEY HOLIDAY

## MISTLETOE MONTANA

SANDY ALVAREZ

CRYSTAL DANIELS

# TANNON

Sensing a pair of eyes on me, I roll over and crack my lids open to find Duke sitting beside the bed, staring at me with his head cocked to the side. Reaching over, I rub the top of his head."Morning, Duke."

Blowing out a breath, I sit up on the side of the bed and stretch, working out the kinks in my back and neck. "Give me five minutes, boy," I tell Duke as I scrub my hand down my face and through my beard as I stand to make my way across the hall to the bathroom. After brushing my teeth and taking care of business, I step out of the bathroom and make my way into the kitchen with Duke on my heels. "Here you go, boy." I open the sliding glass door, and Duke rushes out into the yard as the blistering cold slams into my face. Leaving Duke to do his thing, I go about making myself a cup of coffee. As I'm staring out the kitchen window and watching Duke pounce around in the snow while waiting for the coffee to brew, I make a mental checklist of the things I need to do today. On the kitchen table behind me, my phone pings with an incoming text. Striding toward the table with my cup in hand, I snatch my phone up to see a text from Nash.

**Nash:** Something came up. I'll be a few minutes late.

I shake my head at his text. 'Something came up' is code for 'I'm banging my wife and will be late for work.'

**Me:** Get off your wife and get your ass to the office. You know I have to stop by the site this morning and can't open it.

**Nash:** Fuck. I forgot. I'll be there.

Chuckling, I set my phone down and finish the rest of my coffee. Nash Stone has been my best friend for the past seven years. Nash and I served side by side in the Army during my last deployment. Not having any family, I enlisted straight out of high school and served my country for twelve years. Nash comes from a military family and also joined at eighteen. Both of us have been out for five years. I went back to Washington, whereas Nash came back here, to Mistletoe Montana. Then six months ago, Nash approached me with the idea of us opening our own business. Since leaving the service, I worked for myself doing restoration work on homes I had bought then flipped once I was finished with them. Working with my hands is something I have always loved, and I am good at it. I love taking something old and making it new again. And when Nash asked me if I wanted to open a business with him, I jumped at the chance. I also didn't hesitate to up and move to Mistletoe. Nothing was holding me back in Washington since I grew up in the system. Nash, however, is married with two kids. He and his wife are currently trying for baby number three. His whole life is in Mistletoe. So, six months ago, I loaded up what meager belongings I owned into my truck, and Duke and I made a move here.

I didn't know what to expect when I moved to Mistletoe, but it sure as hell wasn't what I found. The people of Mistletoe love Christmas, and celebrate the holiday year-round. Three hundred and sixty-five days out of the year, Mistletoe Montana is like step-ping into a winter wonderland. I found the town odd as fuck when

I first moved here, but it didn't take long for the place to grow on me.

Growing up, Christmas was not a big deal. I can't remember a single Christmas celebrated in a particular way.

Nash likes to rib me by saying my moving here was fate because of my last name. Fuck if he's not right. With a name like Tannon Christmas, I can't argue that shit was fate.

Duke scratching on the patio door pulls me out of my thoughts, and I walk over to let him in. "Let's get you fed before we go to the office." Duke goes straight to where his food bowl is and sits on his haunches while waiting for me to fill his dish. Duke is a German Shepard, and he has been by my side since the start of my last deployment. When my last tour ended, it took me eight months to get him back. For over seven years, Duke has been the one constant in my life; my companion. "We roll out in twenty, Duke," I tell him, pouring some kibble into his bowl. Duke lets out a bark as if to say he understands before he begins scarfing down his food.

Twenty minutes later, Duke and I are climbing into my truck and making our way into town. The drive to the office only takes fifteen minutes. When I moved to Mistletoe, I rented the house I'm living in from Nash's parents. His dad is a realtor but also owns several rental properties around town. I have been meaning to bite the bullet and buy myself a place finally, but with getting mine and Nash's business off the ground, there hasn't been much time. I kind of like the idea of finding a fixer-upper. I make a mental note to call Mr. Stone and have him be on the lookout for something.

Before going into the office, I head across town to the Wallace farm. Andrew Wallace owns a farmhouse that sits on ten acres of land. He bought the two-story house for him and his wife a few years ago. The couple has been slowly renovating the place, but they had to put the project on hold last year when the previous company they had hired ended up jerking them around.

They contacted T & N Restoration the first week we were in business. Now, six months later, their home is nearly complete. I'm riding out there this morning to make my final walk through and to see if they are satisfied with the job Nash and I have done.

As I make my way down the driveway toward the house, Andrew steps out onto his porch and waves. Putting the truck in park, I climb out, and Duke follows.

"Good morning, Tannon. Hello there, Duke," Andrew pats Duke on the top of his head.

"Hey, Andrew. How are you this morning, and how's Anna?"

"I'm good. Anna's inside fussing with the kids. I'm taking them to the tree farm. Anna wants to get there early before all the good ones are gone."

"Well, I won't keep you too long then. I came to do a final walk-through."

"No problem. Come on in. Can I offer you a cup of coffee?" Andrew asks.

"I'm good, but thanks, man."

Andrew and I spend the next fifteen minutes walking from room to room while I inspect the work my crew finished up a few days ago.

"I have to say, Tannon, Anna and I are pleased with the work you all did here. I still can't believe this is the same house we first bought."

"I'm glad you guys are happy with the results. Was there anything you could think of that we could have done differently?"

Andrew shakes his head. "Nothing, man. I'm telling you; you all did a perfect job. You did everything exactly as we wanted."

Nodding, I smile and offer Andrew my hand. "I'm happy I was able to help you achieve your vision."

"After what we went through last time, you really saved us. Especially since you didn't charge what the work was worth."

I shake my head and go to protest. Andrew cuts me off. "I

looked up price quotes online and asked around to some out of town companies on what they charge. You charged me thirty percent less than what the work was worth, Tannon."

"It was a fair price considering you took a chance on a new business. That and what you had been through with the previous company you paid to do the job. I only wanted you and Anna to have your dream home."

"You gave us that and more, Tannon." Andrew shakes my hand and pats me on the shoulder. "Which is why Anna and I have been singing your praises every chance we get."

"Appreciate that, Andrew."

Andrew falls in step beside me as I walk back to my truck. "I'll stop by your office later this afternoon with a check for the final payment."

"That'll work. I'll see you then." I give Andrew one last nod before climbing into the truck.

As I'm driving through the town square, I take in all the tourists already filling the sidewalks as they make their way from shop to shop. Some have their hands full of shopping bags from Morton's Department Store, and some have ducked inside A Latte Like Christmas, the local coffee shop for something to warm their bellies. I also notice one family wearing their ski gear. No doubt headed for the slopes to spend the day skiing.

A few minutes later, I arrive at the office to find Nash's truck parked out front. T & N Restoration is located directly in the middle of town in a quaint brick building next to a hardware store. The front of the building has a large window with our company name etched on it. It's been six months, yet I still have a sense of pride wash over me every day when I pull into my parking spot to see those letters on the window.

As I walk inside, Duke brushes past me, making his way down the hall to my office to where his bed is. On my way there, I stop at

Nash's office door and rap my knuckles on the open door. "Hey. Got any messages for me?"

Nash looks up from his computer. "Hey, man. No messages. I'm just finishing up on this week's paperwork. How'd things go this morning? Was Andrew and his wife satisfied with the job?"

"Yeah. He said he would be in later to take care of his balance."

Nash nods. "That's cool. Will you be here when he comes by? I need to head out to the lumber yard. That shipment of ours came in a week early."

"Shit. Really? That's good news. I'll call Mrs. Betty and let her know we can get started on her kitchen earlier than expected. She'll be pleased."

Nash stands from behind his desk and throws his coat on. "Sounds good. I'm going to hit the road. There was a tree down on Elk Street, so that means I'll have to take a detour to the lumber yard. I want to get there before old man Cunningham closes for lunch. And you know how he is. He gets to talking to the ladies at the diner, and a thirty-minute break will turn into three hours. Last month my ass was waiting half the damn day for him to return."

I chuckle cause he's right about the old man. "Alright, man. I'll catch you later." With a nod, I turn and make my way down the hall and into my office.

# WINTER

"Seriously, Winter. You missed one hell of a party last night," Brinkley, my best friend, says. "Tammy was caught with her Christmas tinsel around her ankles, while Mr. Claus was giving her a big package if you know what I mean." I throw my head back, laughing. Brinkley has a unique way of telling a story. "She's giving Ho-ho-ho a whole new meaning this year," she says in a fit of laughter.

Soapy water sloshes over the rim of the bucket as I sit it on the wood floor at my feet, creating a puddle beneath my boots. Wearing rubber gloves up to my elbows and my hair pulled back in a braid, I smile. Another day of scrubbing years of dirt off the floors and soot from the two stone fireplaces completed before work. "I hate that I missed it." I sigh. "Hell, between the bar, and this house, I haven't had free time to enjoy any festivities this year. My social life has become nonexistent."

"Christian asked about you last night," Brinkley says, and I roll my eyes. "I heard your eyes roll into the back of your head." Brinkley chuckles. "Come on. What's wrong with Christian?"

"He's a nice guy and all, but..."

"He's safe—too dull?" Brinkley asks.

I plop down on the living room sofa that faces the fireplace and stare at the flames dancing atop the burning logs. "I don't know, Brink—maybe?" I'm even questioning myself. "He's got everything going for him; a steady job, good looking, doesn't live with his parents. The rational part of my brain says to give him a chance, but everything else inside tells me to run the other way. I want more than stability. I want passion—to fall in love. I want that soul-sucking I can't live without them kind of feeling. A man who can make my toes curl just by the tone of his voice."

"You read too many books, Winter. The man you just described only exits between the pages of a romance novel." Brinkley sighs. "I get it—I really do. Hell, to be honest, I want the same damn thing, but how in the hell are we supposed to find a man like that in Mistletoe?"

Slumping against the back of the couch, I lean my head back, and stare up at the vaulted ceiling. "Maybe I'll find him under my tree on Christmas morning." My statement causes Brinkley to giggle, and I laugh with her.

"Tell Santa I want one too. Listen, I got to run. I'll see you at work Peanut," Brinkley says, and I can hear the smile in her voice. It makes me look down at the inside of my wrist. No bigger than a penny, inked on my skin, is a small slice of bread with peanut butter tattooed. Brinkley has the same one; only hers is jelly. She's my other half. I've known Brinkley since we were in diapers. She's my ride or die—my soul sister. Our mommas call us peanut butter and jelly because where you find one, there is the other.

"Later, Jelly," I say before ending the call.

I glance around the room. I still can't believe I bought the Billings Chateau weeks ago. This old American Queen Anne style house has sat here empty and neglected for nearly five years. The bank and the rest of my family tried to talk me out of buying the old place, doing all they could to convince me it was nothing more than a money pit. Nevertheless, my heart was set on it—has been since I was a little girl when I used to ride out here with my grandad and visit his childhood friend Mr. Billings and his wife. They never had children of their own, so the home and land have sat here untouched. It needs a lot of work, but I'm determined to restore it to its original beauty.

I stare at the work I've accomplished so far, taking in the rich mahogany featured throughout the house and the intricate carvings etched into the wood above every doorway. This 1897, 6000-square-feet home has a lot of history under one roof. If these walls could talk, the stories they could tell. That thought alone brings me so much joy. It's not much, but I have managed to clean almost every surface, from floor to ceiling.

A bitter breeze causes me to shiver, reminding me to fix the seals around the front door, along with several broken window panes around the home.

I stand, and lift the bucket off of the floor, and carry it to the kitchen, where I pull my gloves off and sit them on the countertop near the sink.

I pour myself another cup of hot coffee, then grab my coat from the hook on the wall and slip it on. One downside to the home is the furnace is acting up. Sometimes it works—sometimes it doesn't. Not ideal in the middle of a midwest winter, but, for now, I'm wearing extra layers of clothes, using the fireplaces and a small space heater to keep warm when needed.

Grabbing the quilt I found tucked away in an old trunk this morning off the kitchen table, I drape it over my arm and walk across the room to the back door. The crisp December air greets me when I open the door and step outside onto the wrap-around porch. There's snow on the ground, and it's cold, but I love coming out here every morning.

I settle in one of two rocking chairs nearby and drape the blanket across my legs, protecting myself from the cold. I sip on my coffee and listen to the sounds of the river that runs along the property's backside, which I can't quite see due to all the overgrowth.

The Château sits on five acres of land, surrounded by trees and water. It's my own little slice of heaven here in Mistletoe, Montana. My home away from home after years of living with my parents. Not that they minded. Hell, if my father had it his way, I'd live with them forever.

The wind picks up, and the tip of my nose begins to go numb from the cold, so I head back inside. Removing my coat, I toss it and the blanket on the back of a kitchen chair. Cleaning up, I empty the dirty water from the bucket into the sink, wash my hands, then pull the ingredients I need for my mom's famous chili from the fridge and pantry. The sound of a truck horn honking from outside lets me know my dad is here with my new truck battery.

While finishing with the task at hand, I hear the front door open and my dad stomping the snow off of his boots before hearing the door slam shut. "Is that your momma's chili I smell?" my dad says as he strolls into the kitchen. "Morning, baby girl." He comes up beside me and kisses the side of my head—I breathe in his scent. My dad always smells like Brut cologne and black coffee.

"Since mom has been so busy preparing food at the soup kitchen this week, I thought I would have her some dinner already made by the time she got home today."

"Your momma will appreciate the help," Dad says.

"I thought mom was coming with you." I chop more onions.

"She wanted to do a little Christmas shopping at Mistletoe marketplace. You know she likes supporting local businesses. That, and she's had her eye on some new snow globes Tracie had on display the other day." Dad helps himself to the coffee.

There's a pause of silence as I mill about the kitchen. "Thanks for driving out here, Dad." I taste the chili and then add a little extra dash of salt and pepper before placing the lid on top of the stew pot and turning the burner down to simmer.

"Just taking care of my baby girl," Dad says, and I smile. "Now, where are the keys?" he asks.

"Hanging on the hook over there above the potato bin," I tell him.

Ten minutes later, I've bundled up again and walking out the front door. My dad is under the hood of my old red 67 Chevy. I love the old truck. My grandad gave it to me before he passed away two Christmases ago.

I wrap my arms around myself as the winds gust. "Drop the truck off by your brother's shop tomorrow on your way to work and have him change the oil and put a new carburetor filter on," Dad says as he tightens the cable wire bolt. Wiping his hand on a bandana, he steps back and closes the hood. "Oh," Dad reaches into his back pocket and pulls out a white business card. "I've heard about this new construction company in town and that they specialize in restoration projects." He hands me the card, and I pluck it from his gloved fingers. "Give them a call, but make sure you get an estimate beforehand. I don't want to have to bust some heads if someone tries to take advantage of my baby girl."

"Daddy. I'm smarter than that." I stare down at the card and run my thumb across the raised lettering, smiling because the colors are gold and green—Christmassy.

*T & N Restoration.*

"I know you are," he says as I walk with my dad to his truck. He turns to face me. "I'm proud of you, Winter." My dad pulls me in for a hug.

"Thank you, Daddy. I'm pretty proud of myself too."

"As you should be." He pulls back. "Give that number a call. Also, I told Greg you were having trouble with the furnace. He'll be by first thing tomorrow morning to check it out."

"Thanks again, Daddy." I slip the business card into my coat pocket. "I love you." I kiss his cheek before he climbs behind the steering wheel of his truck.

"I love you too, kid." He closes the truck door, and I watch him pull away before retreating inside.

While dinner cooks on the stovetop, I decide to go upstairs for a long soak in the tub. As the claw tub fills with warm water, I remove my clothes and let loose the braid in my hair, only to pile it in a messy bun at the top of my head. Lighting a lavender candle, I sit it on a small table nearby beside my cell phone before slowly sinking into the water beneath the bubbles. "Thank God the water heater still works," I say out loud. Closing my eyes, I soak in the warmth from the water and relax.

I hear the bell on Mr. Jingles' collar as he enters the bathroom. I open my eyes to see him perched on top of the toilet lid, staring at me. He meows. "We survived our first week alone in a brand-new home. What do you think about that, Mr. Jingles?" He blinks before lifting his back leg and licks where his balls once were. "That bad?" I humph. "You're just mad that you've been forced to diet since you no longer have an endless supply of kitty treats and catnip at your disposal," I tell Mr. Jingles, who's the most spoiled fattest cat in town because of my mom and dad. My parents' excuse for spoiling him? Because they have no grandbabies to spoil yet. Honestly, I'm surprised my brother Nick hasn't fulfilled their dreams of grandparent status with the way he spreads his Christmas cheer around town. He's the smooth-talking, tattooed, Harley-riding mechanic of Mistletoe and all the ladies in town trip over their feet for him.

I look around the bathroom, taking in the shellac, and exposed pipes in the walls where pieces are missing. A shriek leaves my mouth the moment two beady eyes look at me from the hole in the wall. "Jesus." I flick the bathwater and suds across the room, trying to shoo it away. Another thing that came with the property —a mice problem. Just another thing to check off my list of people to call. I glance at Mr. Jingles, who hasn't budged. "A whole lot of good you are. Aren't mice supposed to be your natural enemy?" Mr. Jingle yawns, jumps to the floor, and stretches out on the shaggy bathroom rug, utterly uninterested in anything I have to say.

HOURS LATER, THE SUN IS SETTING, AND I'M HEADING TO WORK after dropping off a pot of chili at my parents' home on the other side of Mistletoe. I turn my truck down Main Street.

Everything is illuminated in a warm glow as I drive beneath the canopy of twinkling lights. There is pine garland wrapped around every light pole. Red, green, and gold decorations adorn storefront windows, all of which have different Christmas themes that tell a story of Christmases past.

Christmas is Mistletoe—Mistletoe is Christmas. I don't know any other way to put it. Our quaint little town looks like a Hallmark movie 365 days a year. We're a tourist town, attracting thousands of visitors every year, especially during December. I've lived here my entire life. So have my parents and my grandparents before them.

At the end of the street, I park my truck in front of Whiskey Holiday. Our family-owned tavern. I haven't changed one thing about the building since my grandad passed. Built to look like an old log cabin, it gives the bar its signature charm of an old country Christmas. Climbing out of my truck, I toss my bag over my shoulder. The warmth from the massive fireplace hugs my body as I step through the front door. It's, without a doubt, my favorite feature here. The amber light from the fire casts dancing shadows on the walls as the flames flicker. The air smells of cinnamon and cinder. The exposed beams above my head add to the rustic décor. Beside the fireplace sits a massive Douglas fir, decorated with old-world glass ornaments and bubble lights.

"Hey," Brinkley greets me.

"Hey. Listen, thanks again for coming in a bit early."

Brinkley waves me off. "Don't worry about it. You did me a favor. My mom was trying to set me up with Mrs. Tammy's nephew from Wyoming."

I laugh. "The one that looks like cousin Eddie from that movie Christmas vacation?" Walking behind the bar, I sit my bag down and grab a couple of wine glasses. Like always before we open, I pour my friend and me a drink.

"Oh, before I forget." Brinkley digs through her bag, then hands me the same business card my dad gave me this morning. "You know the restoration Molly had done to the wedding venue down on her farm?" I take a sip of my red wine and nod. "T & N Restoration did all the work. Can you believe they shipped in reclaimed wood from a one-hundred-year-old barn from Connecticut?" Brinkley takes a drink. "Anyway. Knowing you need some home repairs done, she gave me their business card to pass on to you." For the second time today, I look down at the card in my hand. *T & N Restoration*. They sure are making a name for themselves in our small town.

What the hell. So far, two people I trust have recommended their services. Reaching into my back pocket, I pull out my phone and tap the numbers out on the screen.

TANNON

It's getting late, and just when I am about to call it a day, the phone on my desk rings. Picking it up, I answer, "T&N Restoration."

The only thing I hear on the other end of the line is a sharp gasp. I wait a moment for the person to respond. When they don't, I speak again. "Hello. Did I lose you?"

"Um, hello?" an angelic voice rasps in my ear, and I feel as if someone pulled the rug from under my feet, and I swear time stands still. Shaking off the strange effect the stranger is having on me, I ask, "Can I help you, Miss..." I wait for her to provide me with a name.

"Holiday," she supplies.

I smile at her last name. "How may I help you, Miss Holiday?"

"Yes." She clears her throat. "I was given your business card earlier today. I've heard you are the best in your line of work. Anyway, I just bought this house, and I need some work done on it. Well, a lot of work actually," the woman with the sweetest voice I have ever heard chuckles.

"What kind of work are you wanting?" I ask.

"Well, I'm not quite sure. It's a rather old house, and I mostly want to restore the original structure. I'm not interested in making it too modern."

Already feeling interested in the potential new client's house, I sit up a little straighter. I love older homes. They have character. I love everything about restoring the original vision and making it new again.

"Okay. Is there a time I can swing by the house and take a look before going over the ideas you have in mind?"

"Sure. That would be great. How about tomorrow morning?"

"Tomorrow morning works for me. What is the address?" I ask, and Miss Holiday rattles off some numbers and the street name while I jot them down. "Alright, Miss Holiday, I'll see you then."

"Thank you, Mr..." This time she waits for me to give her a name.

"Christmas," I tell her, and I can hear the smile in her voice when she repeats my name.

"Thank you, Mr. Christmas. I'll see you tomorrow."

Hanging up the phone, I rest my elbows on the desk as I try to make sense of why I feel a sudden sense of loss wash over me when our brief conversation ends.

"Tannon?" I hear my name called, and look up to see Nash standing in front of my desk. I must have been in a daze because I didn't even see him come into my office.

"You okay, man? I called your name several times. It's like you had checked out," Nash asks with concern.

"I'm good. Must have been daydreaming or some shit. Long day, you know." I stand and grab my coat from the back of the chair. Duke rises from his bed in the corner and makes his way to my side.

Nash blows out a breath. "I hear you. What are your plans for tonight? I was about to head down to Whiskey Holiday for a drink. Do you want to grab a beer with me?"

Whiskey Holiday is the local watering hole and a staple in Mistletoe. I have been here months and yet to step foot in the establishment. "You know what, man? A beer sounds good."

Ten minutes later, Nash and I are walking into Whiskey Holiday. The heat from the massive stone fireplace wraps around me like a warm blanket. The aromatics in the air: oak, cinnamon, and the smell of the logs burning are inviting, like coming home. Amber lighting, along with colored Christmas lights, set an inviting and relaxed mood, and stress from a long workday leaves my body. Plush couches and leather chairs for seating are spaced perfectly about the large open space. Above my head, I take in the exposed wood ceiling beams.

A waitress carrying a tray spots us and nods toward an empty table in the back corner of the room. "I'll be right with you guys," she tells us.

Duke follows behind as we make our way to the table. The temperature is too cold outside to leave him in the truck, and one of the things I love about this town is most businesses don't mind Duke all that much. Where I go, he goes.

"This place is impressive," I comment as I slip my coat off and take a seat. Duke situates himself under the edge of the table out of the way of foot traffic.

"It is. Winter has outdone herself with it. The tourists love it too. Especially her signature drinks." Nash points to the drink menu lying beside me. Picking it up, I scan it. Christmas Snowstorm Margarita, Holly Jolly Christmas Citrus Cocktail, Candy Cane Vodka Cocktail, Jack Frost Cocktail, Mistletoe Margaritas, White Christmas Martini, the list goes on. "Who did you say owned the place?

"Winter. You'll probably find her behind the bar. She works most nights." Nash jerks his chin and gestures over his shoulder toward the bar. I look in the direction, but all I see is a glimpse of blonde hair peeking over the top of the heads of the people sitting at the bar—our waitress steps in my line of sight.

"Hey, Nash."

Nash gives the waitress a friendly smile. "How's it going, Mel?"

"It's going. This place is keeping me on my toes tonight."

"I can see that. You know how it is around here the closer we get to Christmas," Nash remarks.

"Yeah. Busy is good though, so I'm not going to complain."

Nash looks at me. "Mel, this is my friend and business partner, Tannon. Tannon, this is Melanie. We grew up in Mistletoe together and went to the same high school."

I tip my head. "Good to meet you."

"Same," Melanie smiles. "So, do you two know what you'd like?

"I'll have whatever beer is on tap," I tell her.

"I'll take the same," Nash says.

"No problem, guys. I'll have your drinks for you in no time."

My eyes follow Melanie across the room. The moment she steps up to the bar, two patrons slip off their stools, giving me my first glimpse of the blonde behind the counter. When I lay eyes on her, time stops. As if a magnetic force is bringing us together, the blonde looks up. Her eyes lock on mine. Suddenly, the world around me ceases to exist, and we are the only two people in the room. My heart is about to beat out of my chest. *Fuck!* A woman has never had this kind of effect on me.

*I have to make this woman mine.*

"Tannon, are you okay?" Nash asks.

Ignoring his question, I stand. "I'll be right back." I don't offer Nash an explanation for my sudden departure. My only focus is to get to my woman. *My woman?* Where the hell did that come from.

My blonde beauty keeps her eyes on me as I make my way through the crowd and up to the bar, where I take one of the vacant stools and get a close up look of the woman who will be going home with me tonight.

She stands at around 5 feet 3 inches tall and has honey blonde hair currently hanging in waves over her shoulders. She also has the most stunning green eyes I have ever seen. My mouth waters as I take in the curves of her body. Curves, I can't wait to get my hands on. My hands will be all over that delectable body later.

"Hello," she says, her voice sounding familiar.

"Hi," I return. My blonde beauty smiles, making my dick jump behind the zipper of my jeans.

"What can I get you?"

"Your name," I respond, making her face turn as red as the sweater she is wearing.

"Winter."

"I'm Tannon." I reach across the bar and offer my hand. I'm pleased as fuck when Winter doesn't hesitate to place her small delicate hand in mine. The moment our skin touches, a zap of electricity shoots through my fingertips and up my arm. Shocked by the reaction, my eyes dart up to hers. Judging by the look on Winter's face, there is no doubt she felt it too.

"What time do you get off, Winter?"

I watch as Winter's chest rises and falls with her rapid breathing, and I'd be lying if I said I didn't like the effect I'm having on her. I see the gears turning in her head as she contemplates whether she will take the plunge with a stranger. I can tell right away one-night stands are not something Winter does. The battle is evident in her eyes as she nibbles her bottom lip.

"I normally get off at two, but I think I can get Danny to close for me tonight." Winter licks her bottom lip, and I growl.

"That sounds like a hell of a plan."

Winter's breath hitches at the sound of my voice. "I'll... I'll be right back," she stumbles over her words, and I watch her curvy ass as she turns and makes her way toward a man serving drinks at the other end of the bar. Keeping her in my sights, I watch Winter tap the man on his shoulder. The guy, who I assume is Danny, turns and smiles at my woman. I'm not too fond of it. The thought of any man smiling at her has my ass coming off the stool. Gritting my teeth, I lower myself back down and wait. Why do I feel so possessive over a woman I just met? As fucked as it may seem, it also feels right.

Snapping myself from my conflicting thoughts, I bring my full attention back to Winter, who retrieves her purse from under the bar and places it on her shoulder after talking to Danny. She stops briefly to talk to a slender brunette, whose eyes cut in my direction. She smirks.

*Shit.*

Winter is wasting no time. Locking eyes with me once again, she steps out from behind the bar and saunters my way. I stand from the stool and take her hand in mine once she is within arms reach. "Ready to get out of here before I change my mind?" Winter says as she accepts my touch and I lead us out of Whiskey Holiday. I don't bother saying goodbye to Nash either, but I don't miss the smirk on his face when I look his way and whistle for Duke to follow.

"Is that your dog?" Winter asks when we step up to the passenger side of my truck.

"Yes. His name is Duke." I open the door, and without thinking, I pick Winter up and place her onto the passenger seat. Her breath hitches when I reach across her body and buckle her in. My eyes travel from those intense green orbs of hers down to her full pouty lips. I want to kiss her so badly, but I know once my mouth is on hers, I will lose all control. Besides, the parking lot in front of prying eyes is not the place for that.

"Fuck it," I grind out just before I grip the back of her neck and bring my mouth crashing down on hers. Running my tongue across the seam of her lips, I coax her to open for me. When she does, I delve inside her sweet tasting mouth, taking what I want. Winter tastes of peppermint, and it's addicting. After several seconds I force myself to break our connection, and my dick jumps in protest. "I bet your pussy tastes just as sweet as your mouth." I nip at her lip. "As soon as I get you in my bed, I'm going to find out." With that, I shut the passenger door, leaving Winter looking hungry and dizzy.

Fifteen minutes later, I'm pulling my truck to a stop in the driveway in front of my house. The ride home was silent torture and the air between us is thick with lust. The moment I cut the truck's engine, I'm out the door and making my way to the passenger side where Winter is already halfway out. "Next time, you wait for me to open your door."

She scrunches her nose. "Why? I'm more than capable of opening my door."

"Not when you're with me. From now on, that is my job." I don't wait for a response. Taking her hand in mine again, I tug her toward the house. Winter lets out a giggle at my eagerness to get her inside. Finally, we reach the front door. With my key already in hand, I quickly work the lock. In three seconds flat, I have the two of us inside, and Winter's back pressed against the closed door and my mouth on hers. In a frenzy, we both tear at each other's clothes in a race to get them off. "Arms up," I order, gripping the hem of her sweater. Winter raises her arms above her head, and a growl rumbles deep inside my chest at the sight of her green lace bra with her rosy nipples peeking through, begging for attention. "Take it out," I growl.

At my command, Winter's breathing picks up. I watch as her chest rises and falls with each pant. Doing as I order, she slowly pushes the cup of her bra down.

"Fucking perfect," I say just before my mouth covers her tit.

"Oh, god," Winter cries out, the back of her head hitting the door with a thud.

"Now the other," I rumble.

Winter eagerly offers up her other breast, desperate for me to give it equal attention. "Don't stop," she begs, thrusting her hips against my jean covered cock.

"I'm just getting started," I tell her as I drop to my knees in front of her and quickly unbutton her jeans, then yank them down her legs, taking her panties with them. I toss them over my shoulder, all while never taking my eyes off of her glistening pussy. "Now, it's time to see if this pussy tastes as good as I imagined."

"Yes!" Winter hisses when I grip the globes of her ass in the palms of my hands, bringing her wet pussy to my mouth. I close my eyes and bury my tongue in her tight hole. I lick, suck and fuck her with my tongue until her legs threaten to give out from under her. "Give it to me. Come. I want to taste everything you got." The moment those words are spoken, Winter grips the hair on my head and grinds her pussy down on my face, taking all the pleasure I am desperate to give her.

"Oh, god! Tannon, I'm coming!" she shouts her release.

Not giving her time to recover, I pick Winter up, and she wraps her legs around my waist. The feel of her hot wet pussy against my abs sets me on fire, making me quicken my pace as I carry her to my bedroom.

Reaching behind her, Winter unclasps her bra and tosses it to the floor, then grips my hair, pulling my mouth to hers.

When I reach my bed, I lay her down then stand to my full height. "Spread your legs. Show me what's mine," I say as I begin to toe-off my boots, unbuckle my belt and tear my jeans down my legs. Winter cups her breasts in both hands with hooded eyes and spreads her legs wide, giving me a full view of her slick pussy. Rubbing her nipples, she watches as I rid myself of my boxer briefs, allowing my cock to spring free.

Climbing onto the bed, I settle between her spread legs. Grabbing hold of her right leg, I lift it up and swiftly flip her over onto her stomach. I grip her hips in the palms of my hands, bringing her to all fours. Fisting my erection, I rub the head of my cock through the seam of her pussy.

"Yes." She gasps.

I continue teasing her for a few seconds until she becomes greedy for my cock, and pushes her ass back, seeking relief only I can give her. "Tannon, please."

"Is this what you want?" I ask as I push the head of my cock into her pussy and slowly fill her up inch by inch. I close my eyes and groan. "Fuck."

Wanting to relish the feeling of being inside Winter, I don't move for several seconds. Soon, my need to fill her pussy with my cum takes over, and I begin to thrust.

"Tannon," Winter pants my name. "Don't stop."

"Not a chance," I declare, my chest heaving between each brutal thrust I deliver. "I could fucking live inside this pussy."

Leaning forward, I snake one arm around Winter's waist and pull her to my chest to where she is now sitting on my lap with my cock still buried inside her. I bring both arms around her front and cup her full breasts in the palms of my hands. "Ride me," I growl into her ear. Winter doesn't waste any time following my instructions. "That's it. Fuck yourself on my cock. Take what you need."

"God, yes. You feel so good inside me."

"That's because this pussy belongs to me. You fit my cock like a fucking glove." I grit my teeth and watch my cock sink in and out of Winter's pussy. I can feel my balls tighten.

"I'm coming," she pants.

"Come, baby. Come all over my cock." The moment the words leave my mouth, Winter's pussy clamps down around my dick. She screams my name as her orgasm crashes through her. The moment I feel her juices coating my cock, I grip her hips and thrust into her tight heat, planting myself deep inside, allowing myself to fall over the edge with her.

24

A WHILE LATER, WINTER IS SOFTLY SNORING BESIDE ME WITH HER head resting on my chest as I stroke her hair. The last thought I have before sleep takes me is *this woman is mine.*

# WINTER

I startle awake and blink my eyes open to a darkened room. For a brief moment, I forget where I'm at until I feel the weight of a strong arm draped around my waist, pinning me in place. Glancing over my shoulder, I see a sleeping Tannon. *God, what was I thinking of going home with a stranger last night?* I've never engaged in a one-night stand before, but the moment my eyes locked with his from across the bar last night, I was drawn to him. I continue to stare at Tannon. Oddly enough, he doesn't feel like a stranger. I felt an intense connection with Tannon from the start, a kind of connection that I can't explain because I don't quite understand it myself. While preparing a drink for a customer last night, I felt a pair of eyes on me, and a prickling sensation swept through my entire body. When I looked up, there he was. Tannon. His intense hazel eyes, making my heart skip a beat. Then he stood from his chair, revealing all six feet four inches of pure muscle. Tannon moved across the bar like a lion on the prowl for his prey, and I was his next meal. The closer he got, the more I took him in. His chiseled jawline, brown hair that looks like he's missed his last few haircuts and that slightly curls on top. The way his jeans hug his sculpted thighs, and the way he exudes authority. Alpha drips off this man. All rational thought left me last night. I wanted Tannon. It was all I could think about once I placed my hand in his. A simple hello touch felt like so much more.

Shaking those crazy thoughts away, I carefully and quietly slide out from under the arm, holding me in place. My breath catches when Tannon shifts and rolls over, facing the opposite direction, allowing me to climb out of bed. Once I have my feet under me, I tip-toe across the bedroom while scanning the floor for my bra, which I spot in the hallway.

Just as I leave the room, I stop at the door and look back at the man sleeping soundly in the bed. A nagging feeling in the pit of my stomach tells me not to walk away. I've waited my whole life to find a man like Tannon, a man that I connect with in every way. I took a chance on him last night. Perhaps I should take a chance on him now by crawling back into the bed and letting him hold me. *Just for a while longer.* As quick as those thoughts come to mind, doubt creeps in. What if things become awkward in the morning? What if he wakes up and can't get me out the door fast enough? A man like Tannon, as sexy and good-looking as him, probably has women lined up at the door.

*Sigh.*

*No.*

*Leaving is best.*

Movement in the corner of the bedroom catches my attention. Tannon's dog sits up in his bed and stares at me. *Great.* Even Duke is judging me.

Trying not to overthink my decision, I turn and walk out of the bedroom and down the hall to the living room, where my clothes lay scattered on the floor by the front door. Quickly dressing, I quietly unlock the door and slip out onto the porch. I shiver as a blast of cold air hits my face. Pulling my coat tight around me, I walk to the end of the driveway while fishing my cell phone from my purse to call an Uber.

Luckily, my ride doesn't take long. Ten minutes later, I'm sliding into the back of a car and relay my address to the driver. "Here you go," I hand the driver some cash.

Fifteen minutes later, he drops me off at home. "Have a good night, ma'am."

"You too. Thanks." I shut the door and hustle up to my house, desperate to get out of the cold. Although, when I step inside my home, the temperature is not much different.

When I make it upstairs, I close my bedroom door, turn on the space heater, and shrug out of my coat. I find Mr. Jingles snuggled amongst the covers at the foot of my bed.

I shiver as I rid myself of my jeans and sweater. Mr. Jingle raises his head and yawns. He looks at me. "Don't judge me," I tell him, and he meows as if he understands what I'm saying. "It was just this one time. It won't happen again." I tell the cat, even though I need to say it out loud to convince myself more than anything.

Lifting the flannel pajama set lying at the foot of my bed, I slip it on, followed by pulling on two pairs of wool socks. Next, I go into the en-suite bathroom to wash my face and brush my teeth. I briefly contemplated taking a shower, but for some reason, I like the fact that I still smell like Tannon.

Once finished in the bathroom, I place my phone on the charging dock, noting it's nearly two o'clock in the morning. I only have a few hours to get some sleep since the man with T & N Restoration will be coming out to look at my house today.

Climbing into bed, I pull the blanket up close to my head. Closing my eyes, I try to shut my brain off but find it's no use. Overcome with thoughts of Tannon, and the delicious ache between my legs, how can I forget the past few hours were hands down the best night of my life. Even though it was a one-time deal, and Tannon will have probably forgotten about me by this time tomorrow, I don't regret the passion between us one bit. If I could have one Christmas wish come true, I'd wish for Tannon. On that thought, I fall asleep with a smile on my face and hope in my heart.

THE NEXT MORNING, I WAKE TO THE SOUND OF A POUNDING ON MY door. I blink my eyes open and wonder who the heck would be at my house this early. When I look over at my phone, I see it's just now seven o'clock. It must be Mr. Christmas. Crap! I can't believe it. I forgot about our appointment.

Jumping out of bed, I grab the quilt thrown across the back of a nearby chair and wrap it around my shoulders, then quickly scurry out of my bedroom, stubbing my toe on the corner of my dresser on my way out. "Shit! Shit!" I stumble down the stairs, trying to ignore the throbbing in my foot. "I'm coming! Hold your horses!" I yell.

When I reach the door, I disengage the lock and swing it open. My knees go weak, and my breath catches in my throat. It takes two seconds for him to register the situation. When he does, his easy-going smile vanishes, and anger takes over his handsome face.

"What...what are you? I mean, how are you? What are you doing here?" I ask, finding it hard to form a coherent sentence.

"I think the better question is, why the hell did I wake up this morning to find you gone? To find you had snuck out of my bed." Tannon's nostrils flare as he takes a step closer and leans down to bring his face an inch from mine. "I think I made it pretty damn clear last night that you are mine now. That means when I wake up the next morning after spending all night in that sweet pussy of yours, I expect to have my woman lying next to me.

Especially when I intended to start my day eating her for breakfast."

Shocked at the words that just came out of Tannon's mouth, I stand with my mouth gaped open. "I...I...but."

"But what?" he asks, still in my face.

I swallow. "It was best I leave. You know so that we could avoid the whole awkward morning after a one-night stand deal."

"What the hell are you talking about?"

"Well, I just thought you would prefer I was gone when you woke up. I mean..."

Suddenly Tannon cuts me off. "I swear if you say that word one more damn time, I will put you over my knee. We are not a one-night stand. I claimed you the moment I laid eyes on you from across the bar last night. If that didn't give you the indication that you are mine, then my dick inside your pussy last night sure as hell should have."

At the mention of him being inside me, my sex clenches, and my breathing picks up.

Tannon's pupils dilate, and a growl rumbles in his chest as he firmly but gently brings his hand up and wraps his long fingers around the back of my neck. "I think you like that idea, don't you, baby? Christ, I can still smell me on you," he says, running his nose along the side of my face. "You snuck out of my house and then came back here and crawled into your bed with my cum still in your pussy. Didn't you?"

"Yes," I confess.

"I bet if I stuck my hands down your pants now, I'd find your pussy drenched too."

Like putty in his hands, all I can do is nod.

"Good." He takes a step back, knocking me out of my sexy Tannon daze. "Now that we've cleared things up, I hope we understand one another."

*Cleared up what?* Before I have a chance to question him,

Tannon walks past me, inviting himself into my home. Tannon glances around, taking in his surroundings.

He runs his palm down the mahogany trim around the opening to the living room. The deep color is a stark contrast against the pale grey walls.

"So," I rock back on my heels, feeling a bit nervous. "I love everything about this house. I'd like to keep everything as original as possible. I mean, I'm sure it needs bringing up to code, but esthetically, I want it to remain the same pretty much."

Stopping in the middle of the living room, Tannon turns to face me, his brows furrowed. "Why the hell is it so cold in here? You should have the heat on before you get sick."

"Yeah, uh..." I hug myself from the chill. "My furnace is on its last leg. My dad has someone coming out to look at it this morning."

"You've been sleeping in a house, in the middle of winter, with no heat?" he barks.

"I have a space heater when it stops working, and I make use of the fireplaces as well. It hasn't been too bad." I shrug.

Off in the distance, I hear my phone ringing. "I'll be right back. I have to get that." Leaving Tannon in the living room, I jog up the stairs to my bedroom. When I pick up my phone, I see it's Danny calling.

"Hello," I answer.

"Hey, Winter. I'm sorry to call you so early, but Christy came down with a bug, and I have to take her to the doctor. I won't be able to be at the bar for the delivery in an hour."

"That's okay, Danny. I'll handle it. You worry about your wife. Tell Christy I hope she feels better soon."

"Will do. Thanks, Winter."

After hanging up with Danny, I rush to get ready to head to the bar. Once I finish brushing my teeth and throwing my hair up into a ponytail, I dress in a pair of skinny jeans and an emerald green fleece pullover along with brown knee-high boots.

When I make my way back downstairs, I find Tannon gone. "Tannon," I call out. When he doesn't answer, I walk over to the living room window and peer out. His truck is gone. A piece of paper on the table beside the front door catches my attention. Picking it up, I see it's one of his business cards.

When I flip the card over, I see the note he left for me.

*I'll see you later.*

*~T.*

Okay then.

With a shrug, I gather my things and head out the door.

It's now past midnight, and I am dead on my feet as we lock up the bar, set the alarm, and walk across the parking lot to our vehicles. Without Danny coming in to work the day shift, I spent the whole morning alone until Brinkley clocked in. I filled my best friend in on all the juicy details. Well, not all of them. Some of the deliciously dirty things Tannon did to me, I kept to myself. Brinkley was also the only one who found humor in the mess that is my life when Tannon turned out to be part-owner of the company I'm looking to hire for home restorations.

"Damn, I'm exhausted." Brinkley's keys jingle as she unlocks her car door. "And next time Danny calls in, let me know. You shouldn't take on so much by yourself."

"It wasn't too bad. I only had to deal with paperwork, inventory, and a liquor delivery," I tell her. I also kept waiting for Tannon to walk through the door at some point today, but I don't say that out loud. With the note he left this morning, I figured that meant he would stop by for a beer or something. I was so distracted watching the door every time it opened that I screwed up over a dozen drink orders in a couple of hours. It got to the point my wait staff was looking at me funny. By a quarter to midnight, I had given up on him coming. I'd be lying if I said I wasn't hurt and disappointed.

"I know what you're thinking. I've watched you looking for Tannon all day," Brinkley states.

"Am I that transparent?"

Brinkley laughs. "A little." She tosses her bag into her car. "You'll see him again. If what you told me earlier is any indication, Tannon wants you like Santa wants his cookies."

It's my turn to laugh. "I love you, Jelly." I shake my head and smile.

"I love you too. Which is why I'm giving you a piece of advice."

I throw my purse onto the floorboard of my truck, then look at my best friend. "Let me have it," I tell her.

"Live a little." She looks at me over the top of her car. "Don't go trying to plan a future with the guy. Take it day by day, and simply have fun and enjoy each other. Get out of your head. Throw away the checklist you've made for yourself. Love isn't calculated, Winter."

I let her words sink in a little, but not all the way. "Maybe you're right."

"I'll see you tomorrow." She tells me.

"Drive safely."

"Always," Brinkley slides into her car and pulls away, and I do the same.

Entirely consumed by my thoughts, I'm pulling up in front of my house before I know it. I can't believe Tannon has me so twisted that I don't even remember driving from the bar to the house. It also takes me a second to notice the familiar truck parked next to mine. *What in the world is Tannon doing here at nearly one o'clock in the morning?*

Peering through the truck's windshield, I see the soft glow of the outside light lighting the porch. I also see smoke billowing from the chimney. *Wait!* How did he get into my house?

Gathering my purse from the passenger seat, I open the truck door and hop down. My boots crunch along the snow-covered gravel as I make my way up to the porch. After stomping my feet to knock the snow off, I open the door, and a blast of warm air hits my face. No way is the fireplace heating the whole house like that. Just as the thought crosses my mind, Tannon comes walking in from the kitchen carrying a pizza box and a six-pack of beer. He also looks freshly showered, his hair still damp, has on a pair of jeans, and a dark gray t-shirt. "Hey, baby. I ordered pizza and kept it warm in the oven."

I stand rooted in place as I stare numbly at Tannon. "You let yourself into my home and started a fire." I point to the living room where the wood is burning in the fireplace.

Tannon sets the pizza and beer down on the coffee table in front of the sofa. "I did."

"And, you fixed the furnace."

His lip lifts in a smirk. "The furnace is new."

I scan the room and notice new windows. "I have new windows," I point out yet another thing Tannon has taken care of while I was at work today.

"Wouldn't do much good having a furnace if all the heat was going to escape through the broken windows, baby."

There it is again—that word. *Baby.* It makes my tummy flutter whenever he says it.

"Um, not that I'm upset, especially since you have been busy all day fixing my house, so I don't freeze to death at night, but how did you get into my house exactly. I locked up before I left this morning." I cross my arms.

"Your locks are shitty."

"Okay," I stare at Tannon. I'm finding this whole scene a little unreal.

"Baby." Tannon moves across the room, and takes my purse from my shoulder then hangs it on a hook by the door. He unzips my coat and slides it over my shoulders. "Go upstairs, take a shower, change into something more comfortable, then come back down so we can eat."

"Yeah?"

He smiles, and I melt. "Yeah. I'll be here waiting for you."

A few minutes later, I am standing in my bathroom as I stare at the men's body wash sitting on the shelf inside the shower. I take in the extra toothbrush in the holder next to mine. I smile at the men's razer sitting beside the sink, along with Tannon's deodorant and cologne on the counter. I also didn't miss his dirty clothes placed in the hamper with mine or the jeans, t-shirts, and flannels hanging in my closet. I didn't miss the boots sitting on the floor under the foot of the bed beside my sneakers either. All these things should be freaking me out, but they don't. I like him fixing my house and standing barefoot in my living room while giving me one of his panty-melting smiles. I like that Tannon ordered pizza and waited up for me to come home. So far, I like everything about Tannon Christmas.

# TANNON

I watch Winter disappear up the stairs, and it takes all the restraint I can muster not to follow her. She looked dead on her feet when she came home, and the last thing she needs is me jumping her. As bad as my dick wants to be buried inside her, I tamp down the urge. I feel the moment Winter notices my shit I purposely left all over her bedroom and bathroom. We will need to discuss how things will be between us from now on. Meaning, she is mine.

"I'm starved," Winter finally reappears, coming up behind me in the living room, her hair wet and her face fresh. She's also wearing a pair of pajamas with little reindeers on them and matching socks. Even in her oversized sleepwear covering her curves, Winter is still the sexiest woman I have laid eyes on.

"Come here." Winter fidgets with the hem of her top as she takes a few steps in my direction. I shake my head. "All the way." Winter gives me a shy smile and takes three more steps, stopping directly in front of me.

"Hi." Putting my arm around her waist, I lift Winter off her feet and pull her to my chest. Wrapping her arms around my neck, she lets out a small gasp. I take full advantage and waste no time plunging my tongue inside her mouth. Giving as good as she is getting, my woman threads her fingers through my hair and moans into my mouth—Winter tastes of peppermint and everything I have ever wanted.

Breaking our kiss, I set her back down on her feet. It takes her a moment to get her bearings. "I like the way you say hello," she rasps, gazing up at me with hooded eyes.

"Good, because I plan on greeting you like that every day." I give her one last kiss on the tip of her nose before I grab her hand, lead her over to the sofa, and pull her down between my spread legs. Winter settles back against my chest. I brush her hair aside and drag my lips along the column of her neck, causing her to shiver.

"You want a slice of pizza, baby? I got pepperoni. I hope that's okay."

"Please, and pepperoni is fine."

Using a napkin, I pass Winter a slice of pizza from the box sitting on the coffee table, then hand her a beer before taking a piece for myself. "I can get you something else to drink if you like."

She shakes her head. "Beer is perfect. No other way to eat pizza."

The two of us sit in silence for a few minutes as we devour our food.

"So," Winter starts after she finishes her drink and sits the empty bottle on the table. "I couldn't help but notice some of your things lying around. Is it safe to assume you will be spending the night tonight?"

"Yes." I ball up my napkin and toss it aside. "I'll be in your bed tonight, tomorrow, the next night, and the night after that."

Winter stares at me, her eyes blinking. Adjusting my body, I maneuver her to where she is straddling my lap. I want her eyes on mine when I speak so she can fully understand what I am about to say. "I told you, you belong to me now. From the moment I laid eyes on you, I knew I wanted you. The second I kissed your lips, I vowed to make you mine. When my cock slid inside your pussy for the first time, the deal was sealed. You are mine, and I belong to you. There will not be a night I'm not in your bed or you in mine. Once you have had enough time to realize you are it for me, I will give my landlord notice. In the end, the decision is solely yours. I already know what I want," I finish laying my cards out on the table and wait for Winter to say something.

Finally, she does.

"I think." She looks away as if she is trying to collect her thoughts.

Placing my finger under her chin, I bring her eyes back to mine. "You think what, baby?"

Winter visibly swallows. "As ridiculous as it sounds coming out of my mouth, I think I like everything you just said."

Leaning forward, I brush my lips against hers. "You don't know how happy it makes me for you to say that, baby."

Over the next couple of hours, Winter and I sit, curled up on the sofa in front of the fireplace while drinking beer and getting to know one another.

"So, that's how you met Nash? You were in the Army together?" she asks.

I nod. "Yep. I couldn't ask for a better friend and business partner than Nash."

Winter nods. "I don't remember a whole lot about Nash since he was in high school when I was in elementary, but growing up in Mistletoe, we all kind of knew each other, and I remember my brother saying he was a good guy."

"How many brothers do you have?" I ask.

"Just the one. Thank god," Winter chuckles. "I love my big brother, but he's very protective of me. Fair warning."

I grin. "I think I can handle your brother."

"I think you can, too," she laughs. "What about you? Do you have any brothers or sisters? What about your parents? Are you all close?"

I blow out a breath. "I don't have any family. I was a foster kid. And I have no siblings either that I know of anyway."

Winter gets a sad look on her face. "That's awful, Tannon. No kid should have to grow up without a family."

I pull Winter closer. "Don't be sad for me, baby. Things worked out eventually. I made my way in life, and I'm proud of the life choices I've made." I shift a little. "Look at it like this. If I had not grown up in the system, then I probably wouldn't have enlisted in the Army where I met Nash. I wouldn't have taken him up on the offer to move to Mistletoe and start a business, and I never would have met you." Winter gives me a sweet smile, and I melt a little inside. "I'd say life has turned out pretty fucking great."

Cupping my cheek, Winter kisses me. "Well, I, for one, am glad you decided to move here."

"Me too, baby." I bury my face into the crook of her neck and breathe in her sweet smell.

"Tell me about your business. How exactly did you get started in what you do?"

I shrug. "I've always liked working with my hands. When I was a teenager, I would go around whatever neighborhood I was living in at the time and ask the neighbors to do odds and end stuff around their homes for money. Sometimes it was just cutting the grass, but there were times when I would fix a broken door hinge, or this old man asked me to repair a broken step on his porch. After fixing it, he asked me if I'd stain it. I didn't know what I was doing, so I used the computer in the library at school to research do-it-yourself projects. I learned early on and loved it. I loved taking something old or plain and turning it into something beautiful. That same summer, the old man had me back to help him put down a new wood floor in his house and also new countertops in his kitchen. That was the summer I turned eighteen. A couple months later, I enlisted."

"And when you got out of the Army, what did you do then?"

"I had a lot of money saved up from over the years, and I used some of it to buy an old fixer-upper. It wasn't anything like this place. It was a little three-bedroom house. I lived there while I fixed it up, then flipped it. I moved on to my next project, bought another place, lived in it for a while, and then sold it when I was finished. I was in my third house when I got the call from Nash. I didn't have any roots in Washington, so I took a chance and moved to Mistletoe. Best fucking decision I ever made."

WINTER AND I ENDED UP STAYING UP UNTIL PAST THREE O'CLOCK IN the morning. Exhausted from her day, she dozed off while draped across my chest as the two of us lay on the sofa. Here it is, nearly five in the morning, and I'm still awake just watching her sleep. I feel like the lord dropped an angel onto my lap. If I'm dreaming, I don't want it to end.

Soon, my body gives out, and sleep takes me. As I give in, I fall, holding the greatest gift given to me clutched in my grasp.

WINTER

"Baby," I feel my body shaking and it pulls me from a peaceful slumber. I moan, then prying my eyes open, I lift my head slightly off of Tannon's bare chest.

"What's wrong?"

From across the room, I hear someone clearing their throat. Because I've listened to the sound a million times in my life, I know who it's coming from. "Good morning, Daddy," I say, and take in Tannon's surprisingly relaxed state.

"We tried calling first. When you didn't answer, your mother got worried." My dad says, followed quickly by my mom.

"It wasn't only me who was worried. The big lug here was just as concerned."

Repositioning myself, I sit up and face my parents, both bundled in thick winter coats. Dad's cowboy hat has a thin dusting of snow coating the brim. I notice his stare is solely fixed on Tannon. My mom gives me a warm smile. "We did knock first, sweetheart."

Privacy was the number one benefit to living in a home of my own, yet here I am, in an awkward situation with my parents and a

40

guy I just met. Maybe giving my dad a spare key to the house wasn't such a great idea after all. "Mom, Dad, this is Tannon." I attempt to stretch out the kink in my neck.

Rising from the couch, Tannon holds out his hand. "It's nice to meet you, Sir." My dad eyes him for a second before giving him a firm handshake.

"You too." Dad clears his throat.

"Why don't I make some coffee?" my mom says, then turns toward the kitchen.

"I'm sorry, Dad." I stand then wrap my arms around his neck. "I didn't mean to worry anyone."

My dad kisses the top of my head as he brings his arms around my body. I breathe him in and close my eyes as I always do. "It's going to take some time getting used to you being on your own." He sighs. "Nevertheless, I will always worry about you being out here alone."

"I wasn't alone, Dad." My words come out as a whisper against his chest, and he chuckles.

"I noticed."

I pull away from him. "You mentioned you called first. Is everything okay?"

"Well, for starters, Greg drove out yesterday to fix your furnace and stated a young man was on your property. By the looks of your friend here, I'm going to assume he was speaking of Tannon. Second, your mother wanted to make sure you are all set for the festivities tonight. She is beyond elated, you have the honor of flipping the switch at the tree lighting tonight."

I've been so busy between the bar and this house, I nearly forgot I was nominated by the city council to light the tree. "I'm more than ready, Dad. Tannon replaced the old furnace yesterday. I can't tell you how good it felt to come home to a warm cozy house after work. He also fixed those broken window panes in the kitchen."

"He did, now?" My father eyes Tannon. "What line of work are you in, Tannon?"

"I'm part owner of T & N Restoration, Sir," Tannon replies, and I realize he's still wearing nothing but his grey sweatpants. My eyes roam down his defined abs, following his happy trail until my gaze lingers for a second on his package. *Snap out of it Winter. Your father is standing two feet away, for Christ sake.* My eyes snap up to find Tannon's panty-melting smile looking back at me, and my face heats.

"You don't say?" my dad says, just as my mom walks into the living room carrying a tray with four mugs of piping hot coffee. "Carol, Tannon here is one of the owners of that restoration company Richard was telling us about," my dad tells her, and Mom's face lights up.

"Is that right?" Mom passes me my cup, fixed just how I like it, sugar and lots of cream before handing Tannon and Dad theirs.

"Yes, Ma'am." Tannon smiles at her. "Thanks for the coffee, Mrs. Holiday."

"Call me, Carol." Mom sips from her mug. Stepping close to my side, she whispers. "He's very handsome."

Unable to hide my smile, I agree. "Yes, he is."

"Well, I hate to barge in and run, but your mother gave me a honey-do-list that stretches from here to Polson that needs my attention." My dad sits his coffee back on the tray. "Give this old man another hug." He looks at me, and I step into his arms. "Tannon," he says as he hugs me, "I appreciate you taking care of my daughter and this house." My dad releases me, and I embrace my mom goodbye, then move toward Tannon, who snakes his arms around my waist.

"The pleasure is all mine, Sir," Tannon tells him.

My dad scratches his thick greying beard after crossing his arms over his chest. "How long have the two of you been seeing each other?"

*There it is.*

I was wondering when he would get around to asking that question. I think about lying for a moment but decide against it. Lying to my dad is like moving a mountain. It doesn't work. He'll see right through me—always has.

"Tannon and I met the other night, Dad," I tell him, and all I hear from my dad is a grunt.

My mom lays her hand on my dad's forearm. "Come on, my love. We were young once. Let's let them be." Dad's features soften with my mom's touch, and he looks down at her. She smiles up at him, her eyes full of love.

I've always admired the love my parents have for one another. Mom adores everything about my dad, even when he is less than perfect. My dad calls my mom his little slice of heaven.

I could read all the romance novels the world has to offer and fantasize about the over the top love I find between each book's pages, but it would never live up to the love story I've watched unfold my entire life. Still, not one word, sentence, or phrase could ever live up to the kind of love and adoration like my parents have for each other, and I only hope to find the same for myself one day. My expectations are higher than average because I have grown up surrounded by something much more significant than a four-letter word.

I look at Tannon, who then looks down at me, and I feel my tummy flutter.

*Could I have all of that with him?*

*Is Tannon my forever?*

All I know is my connection with him is far different than anything I have experienced before, and I'm eager to explore the possibilities. Tannon presses his lips to my forehead, and I melt like snow on the first day of spring.

The front door opens, and a cold blast of winter air flows in, and I watch my parents begin to leave. My mom turns around. "We'll see you tonight, sweetie."

"Drive safe. I love you guys." I shiver from the cold, dancing around my bare feet.

"We love you too. Oh, and Tannon, we hope to see you tonight as well, dear." Then my mom closes the front door.

Tannon and I stand silent for a second. "Well, that just happened." I place my coffee mug on the table.

"You have great parents." Tannon spins me to face him with my front pressed against his. Tipping my head back, I look at him and lift my hand to his face, running my fingertips across his beard.

"This is crazy, you know—us?"

"Nothing crazy about knowing what you want, baby." Tannon dips his head and runs his mouth down my neck, and my skin prickles. Tannon's palms skim over my hips before reaching around and grabbing my ass cheeks. My feet leave the floor as Tannon lifts me. I wrap my legs over his hips and feel his erection pressing hard against my center.

"We both should get ready for work." My fingers tangle in his hair as Tannon begins to move.

"We will, but first I'm going to eat breakfast." Tannon carries me up the stairs to the bedroom.


SEVERAL HOURS LATER, I'M BEHIND THE BAR MAKING COCKTAILS FOR a large group of bikers and their old ladies, and I find myself singing along to Bing Crosby's *White Christmas* that's playing in the background.

"Sweet baby Jesus. God spent a little extra time on those men —their women too." Brinkley busies herself, making a Mistletoe Martini for the older lady at the end of the bar.

"Who?" I fill two large glass pitchers with tap beer.

"The bikers," Brinkley says.

"I'm making their drinks now," I tell her. "They're from Polson."

"I need to make a trip to Polson and get me one," Brinkley swoons. I can't blame her. Those men are fine. "Speaking of fine. I couldn't help but noticed the extra pep in your step today, and I'm willing to bet Mr. Christmas is the reason for the jolly mood you're in." I smile because why hide my happiness. "Spill it." Brinkley places the Martini on a napkin and slides it to the customer.

I continue making the cocktails the group from Polson ordered as I tell my best friend everything. After giving her the rundown, Brinkley stares at me like I've grown another head. "What?"

"You've fallen for this guy," she states, and I laugh.

"No. I'm just taking your advice; living a little and having fun."

Brinkley is silent for a moment. "Winter, I've known you since we were in diapers, so don't try to bullshit a bullshitter. You love this guy." My best friend's statement causes me to pause. Hearing what I already know to be accurate takes root.

"Do you think I'm crazy, Brinkley? I've known Tannon less than 48 hours, yet it feels like I've known him my entire life."

Brinkley places her hand on my arm, and I look at her. "Listen to your heart. What is it telling you?"

At that moment, Tannon walks through the door, and the words move past my lips. "Everything."

"Then, there is your answer." I hear the smile in her voice and pull my eyes from Tannon to face my friend. "Don't question fate, Winter." She spots Tannon. "I'm going to get back to work." She winks then walks away.

Tannon sidles up to an empty seat across from me at the bar. "Come here," he says, and I find myself leaning forward. He grips my chin and presses his warm lips against mine, and he tastes like cinnamon. He pulls back, and I lick his taste that lingers on my lips.

"How was your day?"

"Better now," Tannon grins, and I feel my nipples harden.

*Down girls.*

Jesus, the effect he has on me.

"Table 4 is waiting for their drinks." I lift the tray from the counter, and Tannon moves from his stool.

"Let me help," he offers, and I let him take the tray from my hands.

Tannon follows close behind as I make my way to the center of the room. I stop at table four, which sits near the hearth's right side, situated between the warmth of the fire and the twinkling lights on the nearby Christmas tree. "Sorry for the wait," I lift a glass from the tray. "We've been extra busy today."

"Don't worry about it, sweetheart," the biker with grey in his thick beard says as I hand the redhead tucked close at his side her Blue-blue Christmas cocktail.

"Who had The Drunk Uncle?" I lift the mason jar from the tray, and a pretty brunette sitting beside a biker with a tattoo on the side of his head lifts her hand. I place it on the table in front of her. "The Grinch?" I grab another drink.

"Give it to the big guy here with the scowl. I'm pretty sure it was named after him," the biker with long blond hair smirks.

"Shut it, before I shove a poinsettia up your ass," the big bearded biker growls, then takes the green cocktail from me, handing it to the beautiful blonde sitting beside him. I smile at their banter, grab the two White Christmas Martinis from the tray and look around the table, and a petite brunette smiles at me.

"One of those is mine." I pass it to her, and she takes a sip. "Oh, my God. This is so good." She sets her glass on the table. "I'm absolutely in love with Mistletoe. Christmas all year round? I'd never get tired of waking up to all the lights, trees, and Christmas music every day." Her eyes light up as she gazes around the bar. "I can't believe I've lived in Montana all these years and never been here before."

"Well, I'm happy you finally found us. How long are you

staying in Mistletoe?" I sit the two pitchers of beer in the center of the round table, along with empty glasses, and the men begin pouring themselves drinks.

"We leave tomorrow, so we will be home with the kiddos for Christmas eve." I feel a hand on my hip and know without looking it's Tannon's. The petite brunette looks past my shoulder at him and smiles. "This must be your husband."

I look over my shoulder at Tannon, who doesn't correct her. "Oh, um, no. We aren't married." I tell her.

"Yet," Tannon states with confidence, and the men sitting around the table chuckle.

"What is your name, brother?" the older biker asks him.

Tannon steps to my side and extends his hand. "Tannon."

"Jake," the biker shakes his hand. "Why don't the two of you join us for a drink?"

I glance around the bar. Business is beginning to taper, and we will close soon. Tannon looks at me, and I nod. Hell, why not?

"I'll be right back," I excuse myself. Stepping behind the bar, I make a couple of old-fashioned Christmas cocktails, making Tannon's a bit more traditional than mine. After making sure Brinkley and Danny have things covered, I join the Polson crew at their table. Instead of pulling a chair out for me, Tannon pulls me to sit on his lap.

For more than an hour, we sit with our new friends from Polson, who happen to be an MC, The Kings of Retribution. They tell us all about Polson, and we discuss my hometown. We are from different aspects of life. They seem to be rough around the edges and probably have seen more than I care to imagine, while I've led a relatively sheltered, simple life here in Mistletoe. But we are similar in all the ways that count. As I watch them interact with one another, I take in the love each man has for his woman and a strong sense of family at the root of it all.

"What are your plans for the rest of the evening?" I take the final sip of my drink.

"Our women would like to attend the tree lightning later tonight." Logan pulls Bella from her seat onto his lap and places his hand between her knees.

"It's a big event. There will be lots of food and rides," I tell them, and all the women smile, looking at their men.

"Winter has the honor of flipping the switch this year." Tannon rubs my knee. I try to act like it's not a big deal, but I'm bursting with excitement inside.

"You had me at food," Quinn says, then stands and pulls Emerson out of her seat. "Feed me, woman."

Tannon's phone rings and he pulls it from his pocket. "Hello. Perfect." The call ends quickly. "I have a surprise for you." His eyes twinkle as his smile takes over his face.

"Now?"

"Yep," he says, and I slide from Tannon's lap and stand.

"I need to close the bar," I tell him.

"Already taken care of. Danny is going to lock up."

Everyone else sitting at the table rises as well and begins to bundle up in their coats and hats. We collectively walk toward the front door, and my best friend hands me my jacket and bag from behind the bar.

"I'll see you later." Brinkley smiles, and I smile back.

"It was good meeting you all," I tell our new friends from Polson. "I hope you come back for another visit."

"You too. Let us know the next time you find yourselves in our neck of the woods," Jake says as Tannon pushes the front door open, and we step outside into the frigid night air.

The jingle of bells draws my attention.

My mouth gaps open as I stare at the horse-drawn sleigh sliding to a stop before us. Tim, who is one of the drivers for Jingle All The Way, tips his head and grins at us.

Tannon grabs my hand in his. "Ready?"

"This is my surprise?" My tummy flutters again, and I hear the women aww behind me.

"Hell, man. You're making the rest of us look bad," Reid, who is standing at my right with his woman, Mila, says.

"This town inspires me to want to write a small-town Christmas romance," Alba gushes.

"We have got to ride on one before we go home." Bella looks at her man. I watch Logan lift his woman's feet off the ground, bringing her lips to his.

"I'll give you something to ride," he tells her, then gives her a passionate kiss that makes me blush.

"Maybe we'll catch you later," Jake waves goodbye as their crew walks across the parking lot.

Tannon helps me onto the sleigh, then settles in beside me. He throws a heavy blanket across our legs before wrapping another around our shoulders. I snuggle close to his side, seeking his warmth as we start to move. We travel around the town square and along the trail near the frozen lake where families are ice skating. I soak it all in. It feels like I'm looking at the world around me through someone else's eyes. Like I'm experiencing the magic of Mistletoe for the first time.

Sometime later, the sleigh ride comes to an end, pulling up to the towering spruce decorated in beautiful red and green colors. I look around at many familiar faces in the crowd gathered to see the tree lights come on. Tannon steps down, then takes me by the waist, setting me to my feet. "Are you ready to flip the switch?" Tannon brushes the loose hair blowing across my face.

Snowflakes fall onto my face, getting caught on my lashes as it begins to snow. "Kiss me first," I tell him.

Tannon palms my cheek, and I lean into his touch and close my eyes. "Where have you been all my life?" he whispers.

"Waiting for you," I confess. Christmas music playing in the background feels like it's moving through me, keeping a steady rhythm with the drumming of my heart as Tannon kisses me.

This kiss is different.

It's whispering a thousand wishes and promises.

Like long lost lovers, our souls speak to each other.

When I open my eyes, I see more than Tannon gazing upon me. I recognize the father of my children—my future husband—my forever.

The following day after the town festival, Winter and I drove out to Mistletoe Tree Farm. Once we arrived, she insisted I try Mrs. Morgan's famous hot apple cider that Mrs. Morgan serves every two weeks leading up to Christmas. I have to admit, the apple cider was, in fact, the best I had ever had.

"I love this place." Winter closes her eyes and breathes in the strong smell of pine surrounding us. "My dad brought my brother and me here every year growing up. He would tell us to pick out whatever tree we wanted, then cut it down for us to take home and decorate." Winter breaks off a piece of the green sprinkle covered sugar cookie she is eating then slyly sneaks a little bite to Duke. I smile because she does this a lot when she thinks I'm not looking. "Before going home, we would stop at Mrs. Morgan's booth for a cup of cider and a sugar cookie." Winter lets out a satisfied sigh. "The tradition doesn't feel quite the same this year."

"Because you're here with me instead of your family?"

Winter's eyes widen. "Oh, god, no! Bringing you here, and sharing stories of family traditions with you is amazing. I'm just a little sad I didn't get a chance to put up a Christmas tree in my home this year. With the usual holiday chaos that surrounds the bar and working on the house, I didn't have time." She shrugs.

"Well, we can't have that, now can we," I say, lifting her off the ground and carrying her to where my truck is parked.

"Tannon! What are you doing?" she laughs as we stop at the back of my truck. I lower her feet back to the snow-covered ground, and reach into the toolbox, retrieving the ax I used the other day when chopping wood out at her house.

"You are going to pick out a tree, and I am going to chop it down."

"It's already Christmas eve, Tannon. There is no point in putting a tree up now."

"This is your first Christmas in your new home." I pull her body flush against mine and look down at her beautiful face. "It's also our first Christmas together. We are going to carry on the tradition that means so much to you."

Winter falls silent, and tears pool in her eyes. Worried I've done something wrong, I lay the ax on the open truck tailgate and take Winter's face into the palms of my hands. "Baby, what is it? Did I go too far?"

Winter shakes her head. "I can't believe how lucky I am to have found such a wonderful man," she sniffles. "Thank you, Tannon."

"You don't have to thank me, baby. Making you happy makes me happy." I pull Winter's face to mine and gently kiss her lips. "Now, what do you say we go find the perfect tree?"

My woman nods. "Okay."

An hour later, we have the tree Winter picked out strapped down in the back of my truck bed and are on our way back to the house. When we arrive, I cut the engine, hop out, make my way to the passenger side, and open her door. "Why don't you go inside and make some hot cocoa while I bring the tree in."

"That sounds like a great idea!" Winter's face lights up as she hops down from the truck. I chuckle, watching her excitement, and swat her on the ass, making her giggle as she hurries toward the house with Duke on her heels. By the time I walk through the door with the tree in tow, Winter has changed into her pajamas. There is a tray of hot cocoa with marshmallows sitting on the coffee table, and in front of the fireplace, Duke is laid out on a rug with Mr. Jingles curled up beside him.

"Where do you want it, baby?" I ask.

Winter points to the large living room window to my left. "I think there will be a perfect spot." She bounces on her toes, and the smile I've been wearing all day grows.

As I set the tree in its stand, Winter begins unboxing ornaments and strings of Christmas lights. Over the next hour, I stand off to the side with my eyes trained on the beautiful creature in front of me. It makes my heart happy to see her smile, and her face light up with every ornament she places on the tree. Occasionally she hands one to me to put on the tree for those hard to reach spots at the top.

I listen intently, like a sponge, soaking in every word she speaks as she prattles on about all her childhood Christmas memories. Listening to her has me envisioning the two of us making the same kinds of memories with our own children. All these thoughts make it clear Winter Holiday is the woman I want to spend the rest of my life with.

A couple hours later, Winter and I are both exhausted from today's events, by the time we crawl into the bed, but it's not enough to deter me from being inside my woman, and by the way, Winter is currently grinding down on me, I would say she needed me as much as I needed her.

"Fuck, you look good riding my cock." I grip Winter's hips to help guide her movements.

"Oh, god," she gasps, cupping her breasts.

"Pinch your nipples for me, baby." Winter takes her nipples between her fingers, giving them a slight pull. She moans at the same time, her pussy spasms around my dick. Tearing my eyes away from her tits, I look down to where we are connected. Moving one hand from her hip, I zero in on her swollen clit, rubbing it with the pad of my thumb, causing her to cry out. Knowing her orgasm is close, I change our position, bringing Winter's body beneath mine.

The connection between us is lost briefly. As soon I settle in between her spread legs, I reach underneath her, gripping her ass in the palm of my hand, and surge forward, burying my cock inside her once again. Winter closes her eyes and tosses her head back as she wraps her legs around me. She clutches my shoulders, her nails stinging my skin. "Look at me," I growl. "I want you looking at me when you come."

Winter's eyes pop open. Keeping her gaze on mine, I continue to move in and out of her. Feeling like we are not close enough, I lower myself down to my elbows. My chest scrapes against her nipples, and my pelvic rubs against her clit on each upward thrust, triggering her orgasm. Simultaneously, a tingle works its way down my spine, and Winter's pussy clamps down around my cock. Not wanting to break the intense spell we are under, I place my forehead against hers. "Come with me." Just as the command leaves my mouth, the two of us crash over the edge together.

Several seconds of silence pass before Winter is the first to speak. "That was," she's still catching her breath, as am I, "that was...I don't even know what that was. I've never felt so connected to someone."

I brush a strand of hair away from her face then kiss her lips. "We were made for each other."

---

THE NEXT MORNING, I WAKE TO SUNLIGHT CREEPING ACROSS THE room through the window and my woman in my arms. I look over my shoulder, knowing I will find Duke sitting beside the bed, waiting for me to get up and let him out. "Alright, boy." Sliding my arm out from under her head, Winter stirs next to me and snuggles further into the blanket as I climb out of bed. Mr. Jingles stretches, only to curl up in a tight ball next to Winter's leg and go back to sleep.

Striding over to the dresser, I open the drawer and pull out a pair of sweats. Duke follows me downstairs, where I let him outside. From the looks of things, we got a couple of inches of fresh snow. With my thoughts drifting to last night, I walk over to the kitchen table, retrieving my cell phone, and dial Mr. Kent's number.

Mr. Kent owns Mistletoe Jewelers. His store will be closed with it being Christmas day, but he owes me a favor for some work I did for him two months ago. I know he will be more than happy to help me with what I need today. He answers on the second ring. "Hey, Mr. Kent, it's Tannon. I need your help with something."

Fifteen minutes later, phase one of my surprise is taken care of. "I'm walking out the door now, Tannon. I'll have what you asked for dropped off at Carol and Richard's home within the hour," Mr. Kent says, his mood chipper.

"Thanks, Mr. Kent. I appreciate you going through all the trouble on Christmas day."

"No thanks necessary, Tannon. I'm more than happy to help and be a part of this special day. Besides, my wife overheard. She's a hopeless romantic," Mr. Kent chuckles. "Anyway. Give me one hour."

"Merry Christmas," I tell him.

"Merry Christmas to you, too, Tannon."

When I hang up with Mr. Kent, my second call is to Mr. Holiday.

"I can't say that I'm surprised at how quickly things are moving along between you and my daughter, son," Mr. Holiday says after I told him of my plans. I knew Winter's father wouldn't be shocked by my news. After dinner the other night, he pulled me aside for a man to man conversation regarding his baby girl, and that I want to marry Winter. He laid his cards out on the table, and so did I. It was a great feeling when he gave me his blessing.

"It feels right, sir. Like I told you before. Your daughter means the world to me."

"I believe you, son. It will be my pleasure to help you make today perfect for my little girl."

"Thank you, sir."

"All I ask is you make my daughter happy."

"You have my word." With those parting words, I hang up with Mr. Holiday.

"Hey."

I turn around at the sound of Winter's sleep filled voice to find her standing behind me. Smiling, I hook my arm around her waist, pull her to my chest, and kiss her. "Morning," I murmur against her lips.

"Good morning," she returns.

"You hungry? I was just about to whip up some breakfast."

"I'm starved." Winter goes about fixing herself a cup of coffee while I grab the eggs and bacon from the fridge. "What time did you want to head to your parents' house?"

"As early as possible. I told my mom I'd help her cook today. Are you okay with going after breakfast?"

"Sure."

Two hours later, Winter and I walk up the steps to her child-hood home, where her mother greets us at the door. "Merry Christmas!"

Winter embraces her mom. "Merry Christmas, Mom."

"Merry Christmas, Tannon." She pulls me in for a tight hug as well.

"Merry Christmas, Mrs. Holiday. It's good to see you again."

Mrs. Holiday waves her hand in the air. "None of that Mrs. Holiday mess. I told you before to call me, Carol." She gives me a warm smile, and I don't miss the twinkle in her eye that says she is aware of the conversation I had with her husband earlier this morning.

"Carol, don't hog the kids. Move aside so I can hug my baby girl," Mr. Holiday says, coming up behind his wife.

"Merry Christmas, Dad." Winter hugs her dad.

"Merry Christmas, baby girl." He kisses the top of her head.

"Tannon." Mr. Holiday offers his hand, and I shake it.

"Merry Christmas, sir."

"Come on, come on. Take your coats off." Carol ushers us into the house. I take my coat off, hang it in the rack by the door, and help Winter with hers.

"I'm going to head to the kitchen with Mom. Will you be okay here with my dad?"

"Yeah, baby. I'm good. Go on and help your mom." Winter rises on her tiptoes and kisses my jaw before departing.

Once the women have cleared the room, Mr. Holiday turns to me. "Here," he walks over to the sofa table in the living room and pulls open a drawer. "Mr. Kent dropped this by an hour ago." Stepping back, he hands me a black velvet box. Opening it, I look at the ring nestled inside. Mr. Winter clamps a hand over my shoulder. "I want to tell you this now while I have you alone." I turn toward him as he speaks. "I'm glad my daughter met you, Tannon. I knew the moment she brought you home, you were the man for my baby girl. I am damn proud to welcome you into this family, son."

I swallow past the lump in my throat but can't help getting a little choked up at his words. "Thank you, sir. I don't have a family of my own, and it means the world to me that you and your wife have welcomed me into yours with open arms."

The remainder of the day is spent with good food and family. I enjoyed the home-cooked meal, and I even listened to the banter between Winter and her brother while experiencing first-hand what it is like to be a part of a family.

Placing my arm on the back of Winter's chair, I whisper into her ear. "Take a ride with me."

She smiles. "Okay."

Standing, I pull her chair out. I glance over at her dad, who gives me a nod, and then her mom, who gives me a beaming smile and a wink. I even get a nod of approval from Nick.

Winter doesn't ask questions when she notices I'm driving aimlessly around town. She sits beside me, content just being together, which I love about her.

By the time we reach the middle of the town square, night has fallen. With the help of Winter's family, my plan has been put into place. Parking the truck a block away from my destination, Winter and I walk hand in hand. You would think I would be nervous, but honestly, I can't wait.

As we inch closer to the area where Mistletoe's famous town Christmas tree is located, I grow more anxious.

"I wonder what's going on," Winter says, noticing the crowd of onlookers standing around the tree. In the group, I spot Mr. Kent and his wife, Nash and his family. I also spot Winter's best friend Brinkley and her friends who work at the bar. Winter's family came through for me, making sure everyone Winter loves would be here.

"Brinkley is here, and so is Mel." Winter points to her right. "And look, there's Nash."

The crowd parts, allowing us to walk past, and Winter sucks in a sharp breath when she spots her family standing beside the tree. "Tannon, what's going on?"

Just as the question leaves her mouth, the last of the crowd clears, revealing a row of white lanterns, strategically placed, lighting up a pathway leading up to the Christmas tree. Scattered over the snow-covered ground are hundreds of red rose petals. "Oh, my god," Winter gasps squeezing my hand, "Tannon." She's in awe as I lead her down the path, stopping in front of the tree where I drop to one knee.

With her hand in mine, I gaze up at the woman who has become my reason for living. "Winter, the moment I first saw you, I understood why God guided my heart to Mistletoe, Montana. With one look across a crowded room, you captured my heart. Before you, love and forever were just words. Since I held you in my arms the first time, love and forever now hold meaning. Being with you shows me what it feels like to want to spend forever with the one created just for me. If you do me the honor of becoming my wife, I will devote the remainder of my days to making you happy and giving you everything your heart desires. What do you say, baby?" Reaching into my pocket, I pull out the little black box and open it, revealing a starburst floral halo diamond ring. "I love you, Winter Holiday. Will you marry me?" I slip the ring onto Winter's finger.

With tears streaming down her face, Winter nods. "Yes! Yes! Of course, I'll marry you, Tannon."

Our family and friends cheer, and Winter's favorite Christmas song, *Silver Bells,* fills the air. I sweep Winter off of her feet as I stand and spin us around. "You have just made me the happiest man alive," I declare just before kissing the future, Mrs. Christmas.

Four years later

"**D**addy! Daddy! Daddy! Can we get this one?" my three-year-old son, Tannon Jr., shouts as he runs through the rows of evergreen trees at Mistletoe Tree Farm. He stops in front of an eight-foot Scotch Pine.

I turn to my wife, who has a beaming smile on her face as she rubs her swollen belly. "What do you think, baby? Is this our tree?"

"Yeah. This is our tree."

As promised, I have spent every day of the last four years making my wife happy. That includes carrying on the tradition she shared with her parents when she was a little girl.

Now we bring our son to the tree farm to pick the perfect family Christmas tree. Next year will be even more special because our family tradition will include our daughter. I asked Winter to marry me almost four years ago. We were married a week later on New Year's. Eight months after saying, "I do," our son Tannon was born, and our daughter Mary is due any day now.

"Okay, son. If you insist, this is the one." I look down at my son, who looks so much like me, but has his mother's eyes.

"This one, Daddy," he proclaims with a serious look on his face.

"Then, this is the one we'll get." I smile and ruffle his dark brown hair.

"Yay!" Tannon cheers.

"Go stand by mommy while I cut it down." My little boy bounds through the snow, stopping beside my beautiful wife and taking hold of his mother's hand. I pause for a moment and stare at my family.

They are the reason my heart beats. The best of what life has to offer. They are the best of love.

HAPPY HOLIDAYS!